# ROLLER BEARS

## by Eric Seltzer
## illustrated by Tom Disbury

Ready-to-Read

Simon Spotlight

New York   London   Toronto   Sydney   New Delhi

In loving memory of my Aunt Betty
and Uncle Marty Hersch —E. S.


For Sebby and Freddie —T. D.

SIMON SPOTLIGHT
An imprint of Simon & Schuster Children's Publishing Division
1230 Avenue of the Americas, New York, New York 10020
This Simon Spotlight edition November 2020
Text copyright © 2020 by Eric Seltzer
Illustrations copyright © 2020 by Tom Disbury
SIMON SPOTLIGHT, READY-TO-READ, and colophon are registered
trademarks of Simon & Schuster, Inc.
For information about special discounts for bulk purchases, please contact
Simon & Schuster Special Sales at 1-866-506-1949
or business@simonandschuster.com.
Manufactured in the United States of America 1020 LAK
2 4 6 8 10 9 7 5 3 1
The book has been cataloged with the Library of Congress.
ISBN 978-1-5344-7554-0 (hc)
ISBN 978-1-5344-7553-3 (pbk)
ISBN 978-1-5344-7555-7 (eBook)

Roller bears really
love their roller skates!

# They wake up early.

They skate until late!

# Roller bears like red.

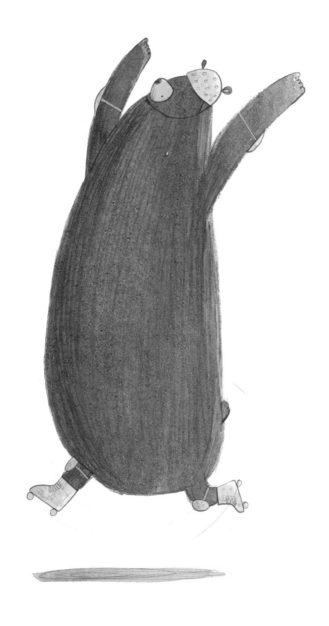

Roller bears like blue.

Some roller bears say,
"Hi, how do you do?"

Hi, how do you do?

Roller bears skate alone.

Roller bears skate in pairs.

When they get tired,
they rest in big chairs.

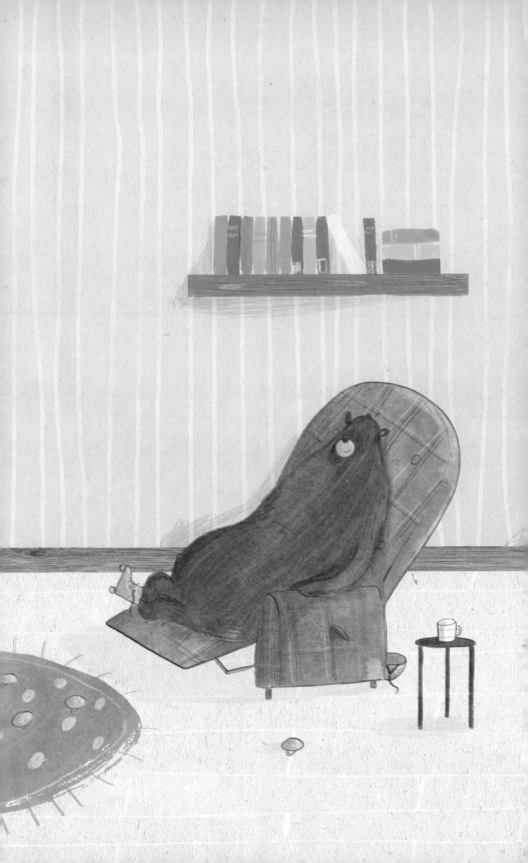

Roller bears
like swings.

Roller bears like slides.

They like old movies.

They like balloon rides.

They all meet to skate
each year in the fall.

There is a party,
and they have a ball!

They come from nearby.
They come from quite far.

Some travel by boat.
Some drive in a car.

One roller bear plans
a little surprise.

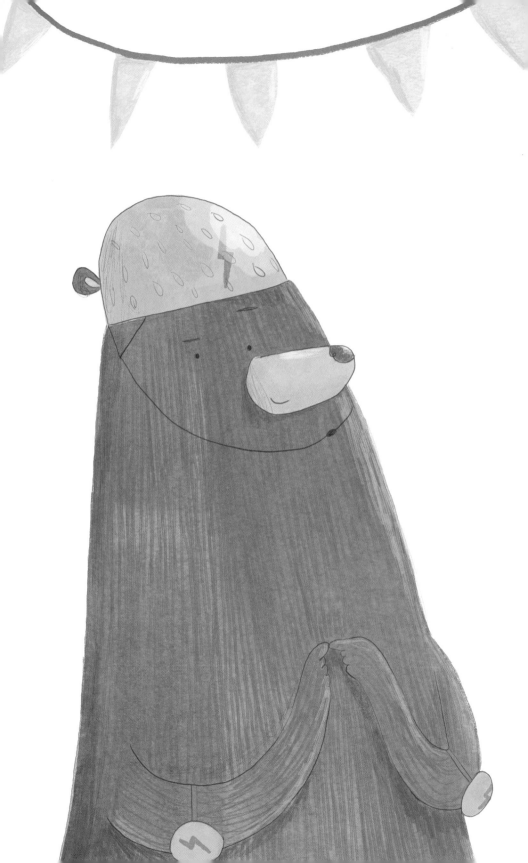

# He made a cake, shirts,

# and even bow ties!

# All the roller bears
# get dressed up in pink.

# Then the party starts

in a roller rink!

Later that night when
they hear a loud gong . . .

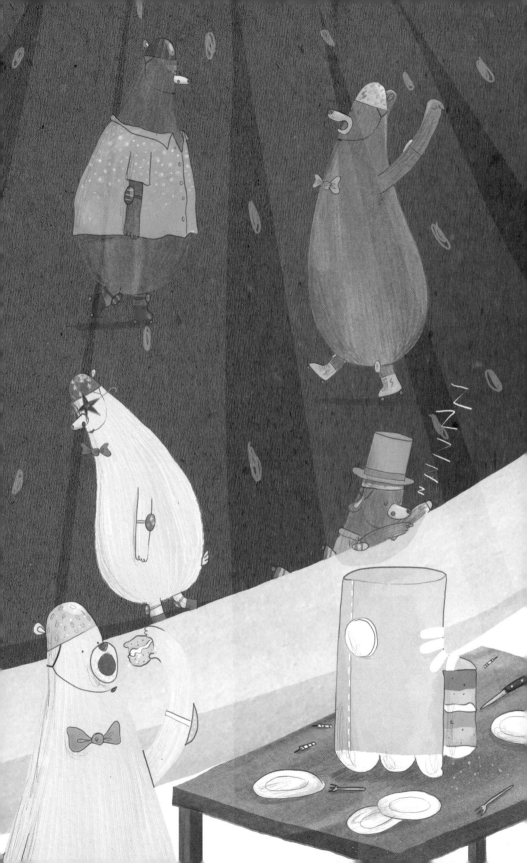

... roller bears stop and
sleep all winter long!